This Book
Belongs to:

wree and cala

RICHARD SCARRY'S
THE GREAT
PIE ROBBERY
and Other Mysteries

STERLING CHILDREN'S BOOKS
New York

STERLING CHILDREN'S BOOKS and the distinctive Sterling Children's Books logo are trademarks of Sterling Publishing Co., Inc.

Published by Sterling Publishing Co., Inc.
387 Park Avenue South, New York, NY 10016
Published in 2008 by Sterling Publishing Co., Inc.
in association with JB Publishing, Inc. 41 River Terrace, New York, New York
On behalf of the Richard Scarry Corporation
The contents of this book were originally published
by Random House in three separate volumes under the titles:

The Great Pie Robbery
© 1969 Richard Scarry
Copyright renewed 1997 Richard Scarry 2nd
Copyright assigned to Richard Scarry Corporation

The Supermarket Mystery
© 1969 Richard Scarry
Copyright renewed 1997 Richard Scarry 2nd
Copyright assigned to Richard Scarry Corporation

The Great Steamboat Mystery
© 1975 Richard Scarry
Copyright renewed 2003 Richard Scarry 2nd
Copyright assigned to Richard Scarry Corporation

Designed by Elizabeth Azen

ISBN 978-1-4027-5823-2

Library of Congress Cataloging-in-Publication Data
Scarry, Richard.
Richard Scarry's The great pie robbery and other mysteries / by Richard Scarry.
p. cm.
Originally published as three separate volumes.
ISBN-13: 978-1-4027-5823-2
1. Children's stories, American. [1. Animals–Fiction. 2. Mystery and detective stories. 3. Short stories.]
I. Title. II. Title: Great pie robbery and other mysteries.
PZ7.S327Rog 2008
[E]–dc22

2007051085

Distributed in Canada by Sterling Publishing
c/o Canadian Manda Group, 165 Dufferin Street
Toronto, Ontario, Canada M6K 3H6
Distributed in the United Kingdom by GMC Distribution Services
Castle Place, 166 High Street, Lewes, East Sussex, England BN7 1XU
Distributed in Australia by Capricorn Link (Australia) Pty. Ltd.
P.O. Box 704, Windsor, NSW 2756, Australia

For information about custom editions, special sales, and premium and corporate purchases,
please contact Sterling Special Sales at 800-805-5489 or specialsales@sterlingpublishing.com.

Manufactured in China
Lot #:
10 9 8 7 6
03/14

www.sterlingpublishing.com/kids

CONTENTS

RICHARD SCARRY'S
The Great
Pie Robbery

Who stole Ma Dog's cherry pies?
Sleuths Sam and Dudley put the
clues together to catch the robbers
and bring them to justice.

RICHARD SCARRY'S
The Great Pie Robbery

Sam Cat and Dudley Pig are detectives.
They find children who get lost.
They catch robbers who steal things.

It was Ma Dog calling.
Something was wrong!
What could it be?

They hopped into their car to find out.

Sam and Dudley hurried to Ma Dog's bakery.
"Where did you ever learn how to drive?" shouted the policeman.

"Some thieves have stolen my pies," said Ma Dog.
Dudley looked through his magnifying glass for clues.
Clues are things like fingerprints that thieves leave behind by mistake.
Clues help detectives find thieves.

"Hmmm. There were two of them. I can tell from their
tracks," said Dudley. "Very fine clues to follow."

"Aha! Look there, Sam! The fingerprint clues go out through that little window," said Dudley. "After them!"

"Please give me a boost," said Dudley.

Ugh! Squinch!

"HELP! I'm stuck, Sam. Do something to get me out!"

"Dudley, **LOOK!**
There go the thieves," said Sam.

"Aha! One of them has torn his pants on that rosebush," said Dudley.
"Aha! They have left footprint clues in the mud leading to that car.

THERE THEY GO NOW!"

shouted Dudley. "I can tell it is them
because they have cherry pie on their faces!"

Dudley is very good at clues.

"Hurry up, Sam. We mustn't let them get out of our sight," said Dudley.

Through the crowded streets they chased the robbers.

"Dudley," said Sam, "maybe we should let that big truck come through the tunnel first."

"Oh I can see that there is plenty of room for both of us," said Dudley.

Crrrunch!

"Now wouldn't you think that truck driver could have seen that there wasn't enough room for both of us?" said Dudley. "I wonder where he ever learned how to drive?"

"Come on, Sam. Hurry! We must catch the thieves," said Dudley.

Sam and Dudley needed a new car to chase after the robbers.
Dudley stopped a car.
"My dear lady," he said. "Please follow that car."
The lady did as she was asked.

The robbers ran into a restaurant.
"Follow them!" said Dudley.
The lady followed them.

The waiter asked them what they wanted.
"Two thieves with cherry pie on their faces," said Dudley.

"I don't know if we have any thieves,"
said the waiter, "but we do have all kinds of other
people who have cherry pie on their faces."

Dudley was puzzled.
How would he ever be able to tell the two
cherry pie thieves from the others?

"I have a plan," said Sam. "One of the thieves tore his pants on the rosebush. If we find a pair of torn pants, there will probably be a thief in them."

"But we can't see torn pants if the thieves are sitting down," said Dudley. "How will we get them to stand up?"

Sam whispered the rest of the plan into Dudley's ear.
"You are a smart planner, Sam," said Dudley. "Let's try it."

Dudley went to a table and asked, "Pardon me, but is either one of you gentlemen sitting on my hat?"

The two gentlemen stood up to see if they were. Sam looked for holes in their pants. No! They weren't the thieves.

23

Then Dudley asked Wart Hog and Baboon if they were sitting on his hat.
"No, we are sitting on our own hats," said Wart Hog.

They stood up to show him.
Sam saw that they did not have torn pants.
They were not the thieves.

They then went to another table.
"Pardon me," said Dudley again. "Are you sitting–"

Horace Wolf and Croaky Crocodile leaped out of their chairs!
Croaky was wearing torn pants!

AHA!
THE THIEVES!

Before Sam and Dudley could do anything Horace Wolf
threw the tablecloth over their heads!

Hurry up, Sam!
Hurry up, Dudley!

Don't let the thieves get away now!
You almost had them!

While Sam and Dudley struggled to get
out of the tablecloth, the thieves ran away.

The thieves jumped onto a trolley car that was passing by.

Dudley caught the trolley car just in time.
Sam caught Dudley just in time.

Tickets, please

Then all of a sudden the trolley stopped. Horace and Croaky ran into their house.
It had strong bars on the windows and doors to keep everyone out.
Now Sam and Dudley had to think of a way to make the thieves come out.

"I have an idea," said Sam.
Dudley listened and said,
"That is an excellent plan, Sam.
May I be on top?"

Sam and Dudley hid behind a telephone booth. Dudley opened his special umbrella. Why is it a special umbrella? Because it is full of amazing disguises! There are clothes in his umbrella that can make Sam and Dudley look like ANYTHING!

Dudley put on the top part
of the disguise. Sam dressed
in the bottom part.
Then Dudley sat on Sam's shoulders.

A lady hippopotamus knocked on the thieves' front door.
"What is it?" asked Horace from inside.
"I have a surprise for you," said the lady.
"Come out and see what it is."

Horace and Croaky stepped
out of their house. They did not
see the trap that the lady
hippopotamus had prepared for them.
"Where is our surprise?"
they demanded.

"RIGHT THERE!"

said the lady hippopotamus.
Sam pulled hard on the rope and those two thieves,
Horace Wolf and Croaky Crocodile, were captured!

31

Sam and Dudley tied their prisoners to the top of a taxi.
They drove back to Ma Dog's bakery.
She would know how to punish a couple of pie stealers!

"You naughty thieves," said Ma Dog.
"For punishment you will have to wash all my pots and pans."

"Oooh!" said Horace and Croaky together.
Maybe THAT will teach them to be good!

And she had an enormous cherry pie for Sam and Dudley. What a delicious reward!
"Here! Let me carry it, Sam," said Dudley. "You might drop it. Thank you very much, Ma Dog."

"Oh, dear! Are you all right, Dudley?" asked Sam.

Wasn't it lucky that Ma Dog had another pie to give them?
"You carry it this time," said Dudley.
Ma Dog waved good-bye to the two great detectives.
They had done a fine day's work.

RICHARD SCARRY'S
The Supermarket Mystery

How is food mysteriously disappearing from Grocer Dog's supermarket? Ace detectives Sam and Dudley shadow suspects to crack the case and catch the criminals.

RICHARD SCARRY'S
The Supermarket Mystery

Sam Cat and Dudley Pig are very fine detectives.
If anyone has a problem, they will try to solve it.
Grocer Dog telephoned to tell them that he had a problem.

Sam and Dudley drove to Grocer Dog's supermarket to see if they could solve it.

Dudley parked the car outside the supermarket.
My! Where did Dudley ever learn how to drive?

Grocer Dog told Sam and Dudley that someone had been stealing food from his supermarket. The only way out was through the check-out counter.

Someone had been sneaking food out of the store without paying for it.

"It's a mystery to me how they do it," said Grocer Dog.

44

"Then we will find out," said Dudley.
"But first we must put on our disguises.
We don't want the robber to know who we are."

Sam and Dudley went into Grocer Dog's private office. Dudley always keeps disguises in his umbrella. Whenever he and Sam want to look like someone else, they put on costumes from Dudley's umbrella.

Just look at that nice lady shopper coming out of Grocer Dog's office!
And what is that in her shopping cart? Why, it is a sack of potatoes!

You wouldn't know that was Sam and Dudley, would you? Now don't tell anyone!

"Keep your eyes and ears open," Dudley said to Sam Potatoes.
"The robber is probably stealing food this very minute."

"Cootchie coo," said Dudley.

"What a cute little baby bunny! But you are much too thin.
Your mother should feed you more to fatten you up."
"That's not a baby bunny, Dudley," said Sam Potatoes.
"It's a bunny doll."

A few minutes later Dudley said,
"SAM! I have solved the mystery!
I know how the robber steals!
Look! There she is now!"

This is what Dudley saw.
Can you tell which one is
the thief? Are you sure?

Dudley rushed across the supermarket.
He grabbed a lady's hat off her head and smashed it to the floor.

"I've got you now!" he shouted.
"That's not make-believe fruit on your hat.
It's REAL fruit and you were going to steal it!"

"Just you look!" said the lady.
"You have ruined my new hat!
You think you're so smart!
Here! You just eat one
of these REAL apples!"

Dudley took a bite of the apple.
It was not a real apple.
It was made of cloth.
And it was stuffed with feathers!

Poor
Dudley!

Dudley was sorry that he had ruined the lady's hat.
To show everyone that he was really a nice lady,
he helped Mother Bunny pick out a watermelon that
she couldn't reach.

"Now please try to catch this one," said Dudley.

Meanwhile Sam Potatoes was keeping
his eyes and ears open.

"Dudley," said Sam.
"Did you notice how FAT that bunny doll is getting?"

Dudley was not paying too much attention to what Sam was saying.

"Sam, look!" he shouted. "There's the robber! This time I'm sure of it!"

Dudley ran off through the store.

A lady shopper wished to buy a sack of potatoes.
Sam Potatoes escaped from her just in time.

"That lady crocodile is the robber!" said Dudley.
"She is hiding stolen food in her baby carriage."

54

Dudley smashed into the baby carriage.
But there was no stolen food inside it.
Mother Crocodile was furious!

"Just when I finally get my darling little babies to sleep,
you have to come along and awaken them!" she said.
"Dudley! Dudley! I could have told you she wasn't the thief!"
said Sam Potatoes. "I know who is doing the stealing!"

For once Dudley paid attention.
"Who is it?" he asked. "How do you know?"

"There is no time to explain now," said Sam.
"The robber has to leave by way of the check-out
counter. Hurry there! It's that lady with…

Before Sam could finish talking —**Sploshhh!**

Dudley landed in a pickle barrel!
Sam landed on his head.
Sam was knocked unconscious!

"How dare you call ME fat?" said the lady.
"And where did you ever learn how to drive?"

But look! Someone is picking up a sack of potatoes!

Suddenly Dudley noticed that Sam was missing.

"Sam knows who the robber is. I must find him," said Dudley.
He asked the fat lady, "Where is my sack of potatoes?"

"A bunny lady took it to the check-out counter," she said.

Dudley rushed there, but the bunny lady didn't have Sam Potatoes. Mother Bunny was saying to Grocer Dog, "I have decided not to buy any food today, after all."

CHECK-OUT COUNTER

Grocer Dog replied, "That's what you say every day, Madam."

Dudley took a closer look and wondered, "But how does she feed her baby bunny?"

Then suddenly he remembered what Sam had said earlier: "That's not a baby bunny. It's a bunny doll."

And my! That doll had grown very, very FAT!

"STOP THIEF!" cried Dudley as he leaped out of his disguise. "Your bunny doll is stuffed with stolen groceries!"

Mother Bunny was the thief!

BUT NO! It was not a mother bunny at all!
The thief was Blackfinger Wolf,
the wicked supermarket robber!
He had been wearing a bunny disguise.
He threw his bunny mask away.

Out of the supermarket the robber fled.
Dudley didn't have time to look for Sam.

He had to catch Blackfinger Wolf all by himself.

Hurry, Dudley!

Down into the lower part of town,
down where all the robbers lived,
Blackfinger Wolf rolled into his robber's den.

Dudley rolled after him...

...right into a trap!

Poor Dudley!
"Oh! I wish Sam was here," he moaned.

Just then the doll began to move and walk.
"HELP!" screamed Blackfinger.
"The doll is alive!

HELP! SAVE ME!"

68

Blackfinger let go of the rope and started to run away.

Crrrump!

Dudley landed on top of him.
But Dudley was afraid of the doll, too!
"HELP! SAVE ME!" he shouted.

The doll stopped in front of him.

Zzzip!

Out of the doll stepped a sack of potatoes.
And out of the sack of potatoes stepped Sam!

"SAM! It's you!" said Dudley happily.
"DUDLEY! It's you!" said Sam. "But how did I get here?"

Then Dudley explained. "Your disguise was so good that
Blackfinger Wolf thought you were really a sack of potatoes.
When you were knocked unconscious, he stole you, too!"
"He was a very clever thief," said Sam.
"But we are very clever detectives, aren't we?" Dudley grinned.

RICHARD SCARRY'S

The Great Steamboat Mystery

When did Mrs. Pig's fabulous pearl necklace go missing? Crime-solvers Sam and Dudley search a steamship for the light-fingered jewel thieves.

RICHARD SCARRY'S
The Great Steamboat Mystery

JUST MARRIED

Mr. and Mrs. Pig just got married.
They invited all their friends to a big wedding party aboard the steamboat *Sally*.
Just for fun they asked everybody to wear a costume.
Mr. Pig also asked Sam and Dudley, the famous detectives, to come to the party.
He wanted them to see that no wedding presents got stolen.
Sam and Dudley wore costumes, too. They dressed like pirates.

"We must keep an eye on all the guests," said Pirate Sam.
"A jewel thief is certain to sneak aboard in all this crowd."

When everyone was on board, the ship left the dock for a happy wedding party.

Sam and Dudley stopped to check with Mr. Pig.
"Shhh," said Mr. Pig. "Mrs. Pig is taking a nap in her deck chair.
Just look at the beautiful pearl necklace she received as a wedding present."

Mr. Pig's favorite present was a gold pocket watch with an alarm.
He could set the alarm for any time and it would make a loud B-R-I-N-G!
when that time came around.

"You must be careful that your presents do not get stolen,"
said Sam, as they went off to the dining room to see if everything
was ready for the party. They left Mrs. Pig snoozing all alone on deck.

While Mrs. Pig was sleeping,
a pair of scissors suddenly appeared.

Snip!

The scissors cut her string of pearls.
Then two hands covered with white
powder grabbed for the pearls as they
slipped off the string. White powder
flew all over Mrs. Pig's dress.

When she woke up she found, to her horror, that her pearls
were missing. She ran into the dining room, screaming,
"My pearls! My pearls! They have been stolen!"

"Whoever stole your pearls has gotten white powder all over your dress,"
said Sam. "The thief must have been covered with some sort of white powder.
That clue should help us find the thief."

"Don't worry, Mrs. Pig," said Dudley. "We will find your pearls. Come, it's time
to cut the cake."

The ship's baker brought in the wedding cake.
"Look!" said Dudley. "He is covered with white powder."
"It's white flour," said Sam. "We had better keep an eye on him."

The bride and groom cut the wedding cake.

All the guests sat down to eat a piece of the cake.
Each piece had a prize baked into it.
Mrs. Pig's prize was a pair of glass earrings.

"Hmm," whispered Sam. "The thief will try to smuggle
Mrs. Pig's pearls ashore when the wedding party is over.
We must watch what the baker takes with him. He might
try to hide the pearls in another cake."

A little baby sat at one of the tables with his nursemaid.
He was feeding cake to his toy duck. "Isn't he cute?" said Dudley.
"Yes," said Sam. "But why is he covered with white powder?"
"Oh, he is such a little rascal," the nursemaid explained.
"He knocked over a can of talcum powder while I was changing
him this morning and he got it all over himself."

"Goo, goo," said the baby.
"Quack, quack," said the duck.

"Well, we must get to work," said Sam.
"Let's go out on deck. We might find
some white-powder clues there."

On deck they saw a suspicious-looking lady pirate.
She was covered with white powder and carrying a treasure chest.

"I'll bet Mrs. Pig's pearl necklace
is hidden in that chest," said Dudley.
"Hurry! We must stop her before
she hides it somewhere."

Dudley came rushing around the corner just as the lady pirate
was putting down her chest. He was going too fast to stop.

Ouch! His pirate sword rammed into her.
She screamed, leaped into the air...

... and over the side she went.
Dudley jumped right in after her.

"I will have the captain stop the boat," shouted Sam.

Dudley grabbed the lady pirate and her treasure chest. Then Sam and two sailors hauled them aboard.

The lady pirate was furious. "You have ruined my sugar doughnuts," she said. "Now they are all wet."

"Sugar doughnuts! That is where the white powder came from," thought Sam. But he was still suspicious. She could be hiding the pearls somewhere else.

As Sam and Dudley walked along the deck, they suddenly
saw white powder blowing through the slats of a door.

They tried to open the door. It was locked.
"Break down that door, Dudley!" shouted Sam.

Dudley smashed down the door. There sat a lady powdering her nose in front of a breezy porthole. She jumped up and tried to escape.

"STOP, THIEF!" shouted Dudley.

The lady stopped. She had to. She was stuck in the porthole. Sam and Dudley pulled and pulled...

...until the lady came unstuck.

"Why did you try to escape from us?" asked Sam.
"Well, wouldn't *you* try to escape if two pirates came smashing through your door?" she answered.

"I didn't see any pearls on her," said Dudley as they walked away.
"She *could* be the thief, though," said Sam. "She was covered with white powder."
"Yes," Dudley agreed. "And that giant-size powder puff was very suspicious. We had better keep an eye on her."

91

"Look!" said Sam. "Someone has left a trail of powder along the deck.
It may lead us to the thief."
"Stay out of our way, Little Rascal," said Dudley.
"We are trying to solve a mystery."

As they followed the trail, Dudley saw the baker in the kitchen, baking another cake.
The lady pirate was sitting by her chest, eating soggy sugar doughnuts.

Mrs. Pig was still crying over her lost pearls.
Mr. Pig was waiting for his watch to go B-R-I-N-G!

"We must find out where those pearls are
hidden," said Sam. "But how do we go about it?"

"Aha!" cried Dudley. "The trail of
powder is leaking from this keg.
Maybe *this* is the big clue we need."

Boom!

Dudley and Sam suddenly flew into the air.
One of the guests was using the white gunpowder to shoot his toy cannon.

"Well, that was certainly a *noisy* clue," said Dudley.
"Right," answered Sam. "And it gives me an idea.
I think we should set a noisy *trap* to help us catch the thief."

They rushed back to Mr. Pig.
"I want to leave your watch where the thief can steal it," said Sam.
"By using it for a trap, we will be able to find Mrs. Pig's pearls
when the thief tries to smuggle them off the ship."

Mr. Pig agreed, though he was afraid he might lose his watch, too.

Sam left the watch on deck—in plain view.
"Now let's get out of sight so the thief can steal it," he said.

Sure enough! When they returned a few minutes later, the watch was gone...
But there were white-powder marks on the deck—right where the watch had been.

"My trap worked," said Sam. "Now all we have to do is wait
until people start to go ashore. We are coming into dock now."

As the guests gathered on deck, the ship's baker
appeared with a freshly baked cake.
"Aha!" said Dudley. "There is the thief and I know where
he has hidden the watch and necklace. Just watch me!"
He sliced furiously into the cake with his sword—
but there wasn't a thing hidden inside it!

The baker was furious. But since his cake was ruined
there was nothing to do but offer everyone a piece.

Little Rascal took a big piece of cake and walked away, pulling his duck behind him.
As it rolled along, the duck started to lay tiny white eggs.
"What a clever toy!" said Sam. Suddenly... B-R-R-I-I-N-N-G-G!

A loud alarm went off.
The duck jumped. Everyone jumped.

"Those eggs! They're not eggs!" Sam shouted. "They're pearls. And in a minute that duck is going to lay a gold pocket watch! Don't let those thieves get away!"

Little Rascal picked up his duck and ran.
His nursemaid followed him.
They crashed right into the lady pirate.

Everyone began to slip on the rolling pearls and before they knew it...

...overboard they all went!

SPLASH!

SPLASH!

POP!

Little Rascal fell right into Sergeant Moriarty's lap.

"Arrest that baby!" Sam shouted. "He is a jewel thief."
"Why, bless my soul!" exclaimed Police Sergeant Moriarty.
"It's not a baby! It's Raffles Rat, the notorious jewel thief.
And there is his partner, Four-Finger Fox, hanging from our mast.
I've been looking all over for these thieves.
I'm going to take them for a nice ride down to the police station
after I rescue those poor swimmers."

Dudley! Can't you get that duck to stop ringing?

BRINNNGG!

When everyone was safely back on board, they all started scrambling around to pick up the pearls and return them to Mrs. Pig.

She restrung them with thread and put them around her neck. She was happy once again.

Dudley made the duck lay a gold pocket watch so Mr. Pig was happy, too.

"How did you think of setting the trap with the watch?" Mr. Pig asked Sam.

"Well," said Sam, "I knew that the thief had to smuggle the pearls off the ship, but I didn't know where he would hide them. I decided that, if I could get him to steal the watch, he would have to hide that, too.

"But before I left the watch on deck, I set the alarm to go off at the time the boat would be landing. When I heard the alarm go off, I knew right away who the thief was."

"I must say," added Dudley, "that Little Rascal was very clever to dress up in baby clothes. Who would think that a baby could be a jewel thief?"

Mr. Pig thanked Sam and Dudley and paid them well for their clever detective work.

Mrs. Pig gave each of them a dozen big hugs and kisses to show her thanks.

As for Little Rascal and his partner, Sergeant Moriarty put them in jail, where they belonged.